I was there and not anymore

Emcee Ferrer

Ukiyoto Publishing

All global publishing rights are held by

Ukiyoto Publishing

Published in 2024

Content Copyright © Emcee Ferrer

ISBN 9789361726392

Dedication

To all the brave hearts that holds all the pieces of their heart after it got broken, you will get pass through it.

To Zii, for reminding me of how bright I shine whenever I write. This book won't come alive without you.

To Alfred A., for being my soul mate and being the most wonderful gift from the universe.

To my family who has been with me with and without distances.

To Harlyn, I made it, so you should too.

To my creator, for putting fire in my heart and soul.

To him, for breaking me into pieces,

and

to myself for using those broken pieces into something beautiful.

Contents

I. I was there

Castles

Come back
were the first two words
I have thought when
the castles we built out of sand and dreams
were slowly getting washed away
by waves.
Come back,
but you never did.

Everything we were and we weren't

We were happy,

We were together,

We were as one,

You were the sugar to my coffee,

The peanut to my butter,

You were the sun to my cloudy days,

You were the comfort to my tiring times,

You were the smile on my lips,

I was the magic to your spell,

the chaos to your order,

I was the runner when you were running away,

We were drifting apart,

yet we were love –

We were love,

We were the main game,

but we weren't the end game

We were everything

but now we weren't.

Memories

How does one forget when the roots had been planted so deep?

Memories always come but they never go. They never leave its host.

Once it has made its comfort to the core of you, it'll never leave you.

Memories always come but they never go. We will always remember them.

Forget at times—yes, but we never fully forget them

because memories never go – we only choose to hide them – some of them,

and now I desperately wonder as to how I can forget the memories you have

planted in me when its roots are ingrained deep connecting to you?

One never forgets. One only chooses to bury things they deem unimportant.

And I can never forget you but I choose to bury you along with the memories.

A little not over you

I have said to myself that I have moved on

but on some days, I still think about you.

I started drinking coffee because I told myself

"I was over you"

but on some days, the coffee tastes just like you.

I indulge myself with books for I am coming back to
my hobbies

but on some days, the main lead looks just like you.

I began to go out and have fun because I thought

"I have broken free from your shadows"

but on some days, the clubs are just filled by your
images.

When on some days I feel like a strong and
independent woman devoid of romances in life,

The strings of your memories are pulling me back

reminding me of how wonderful your touches are –
of how marvelous it is to be touched

When on some days I made myself strongly believe
that you don't matter,

your shadow veils over me as a constant reminder of
how much I can never forget you

And when I began to breathe just fine because I have truly believed that I was over you,

Small details would whisper to me to remind me of you and –

Little did I know that I was a little not over you.

On some days, it feels like I can conquer the world
without you

but on most days, it feels like I'll never get over you.

Remnants of the war

We were at war – as I could remember.

There weren't gun fires or bombs flying away, instead

there were silences and explosions of feelings.

We fought so hard to keep what we had.

I fought so hard to keep you

and

you fought with your best to protect yourself.

I lost the war, but you won your battle.

Now, you are just nothing, but a remnant of the war

that will keep me reminding of why I lost you.

Being with you is the second best thing in my life –
Finding you was the best thing –
Now, forgetting you will be the better one among the
three.

Option

I remember the night when you held my hand and told me that there were greater things to be pursued, and I am not one of them.

Then, you taught me that people will always have options. People will always choose what they reckoned to be important for them.

And that was the day I've learned that with you, I'm one of your many options but will never be your choice.

Someday, I'll stop.

Someday, I'll stop looking for you in the sea of stars.

Someday, I'll stop waiting for you every time the sun comes down.

Someday, I'll stop yearning for your warm embrace in the brightest light of the moon.

Someday, I'll stop filling the rivers with tears from my eyes.

One day my heart will start putting bandages on itself.

One day my eyes will be filled with the stars I used to elude.

One day my arms will fill the ghost of your touches.

One day I'll sail through river and seas.

and

Someday, I'll stop loving you

for

one day, I'll start loving myself.

Nothing is more painful than a man being confused
with his feelings for you.

It was a yes, then a maybe.

We could be, and then we might not be.

You were here, and then you weren't.

It was love, then pity.

It was me, then her.

At 3 a.m.

I wouldn't be out here crying

if

you weren't confused with your feelings.

Moon

Of many things, the moon holds so many memories of you and me.

The moon is an undying witness of our love and loss.

We love with the moon and lost each other by the moon.

The moon is a confidant who knows of how much love we have for each other.

The moon saw us naked with the truth and covered with lie.

The moon holds many memories of you and me.

And unlike you,

The moon has been constant.

I go back to our memories

not because I haven't moved on

but because

I need words and emotions to write.

I never knew the word in   complete

not until you left me

Incomplete

Fears

I'm scared of heights.

My stomach churns when I take at least one step higher than I already am,

but when you lifted me up making me feel high with your love I didn't mind.

I'm scared of the elevators.

I couldn't stand staying inside closed spaces as it threatens the freedom of my body,

but every time you keep me inside your arms I don't mind.

I'm scared of the dark.

I hate the idea of not being able to see things around me,

but when I blindly followed you around I didn't mind.

I'm scared of being left out,

It takes the very breath of my soul which makes me gasp for air

so when you did, I didn't know what to do because everything started to fall apart.

I'm scared of many things before you, but I was never scared of you.

After you, I was not scared of anything anymore

except that I am scared of love now.

Because I might never fall in love the way I used to love you.

And maybe you're the ending,
I don't know how to begin.

And tonight, I'll weep for my loss,
for you are something which I will regret
not having.

You are a bad habit
I've always wanted to get rid of
but could never do.

On

my

worst

nights

I

just

lay

and

cry

I was there and not anymore

Only with my

disappearance

shall you know the true meaning of love.

It has been long gone

but at some point I am still hoping and wishing for it
to

come back.

Accountability

If I could teach you one thing, it would be accountability.

I will teach you about the essence of taking responsibility of something you decided to own

and knowingly broke it.

I will tell you that once you have taken something in, it'll be your sole responsibility to take care of it –

that if you didn't want it anymore, you need to return it as it was.

I will teach you about the idea of how a broken one could never fix itself

because once something is broken you could never restore it the same way it used to be.

If I could write an ending, it wouldn't be
yours and mine.

The world is unfair
for letting you break me
and making me fix what you've broken.

If parallel universe is real,

I hope I have your heart as you have mine.

Intrusive thought

All this time, I know under the deepest thoughts I
have, I haven't moved on because I haven't seen you
more miserable than I am.

Just like how I hope for the rain to stop,
I'm keeping my hopes for
my heart to stop beating
your name.

I guess I just loved you
way too much that I –
cannot bring my heart
to love another one
of you.

It was like remembering the smell of the perfume you
used to smell,

tasting the dessert you used to eat,

recalling the characters from the book you've read,

reminiscing the lines from the movie you've watched,

It was like thinking of what you were supposed to say
a few minutes back

but can't.

just like that –

I still think about you even if I can't remember your
name – anymore

somewhere, somehow, the letters are gone

but the feelings were kept.

I didn't only build sand castles.

I built your dreams on top of mine.

I made promises of dreams in our life together

but you chose to bury those along with my sandcastles.

I still look for your smell in
the embrace of another –
I still feel your touch in
the hands of another –
I still look for your soul in
the eyes of another –

Where are you?

Dear you,

Do you ever miss me?

Do you also look for me in the embrace of others?

Do you also weep at night and recall our memories?

Do you also recoil from the pain of losing me?

Do you think of me whenever you smile?

Do you also ask yourself if it was right to let go of me?

Do you also wonder if how I'm doing?

Do you ever think of me even just for a single minute of your day?

or

Did you already find a new kind of embrace?

Do you already miss someone else?

Do you already spend your night making new memories?

Did you already find your answer for letting me go?

Did you already find someone to spend every single time of your day?

As for me,

I wouldn't be here writing these things

if I have already let go of you –

at least not the feelings, yet.

Unraveling

I am still trying to unlove you.

I am trying to undo the wretched hell

  you've put me through.

I am still completing the missing puzzle I've become
because you took one piece away.

I am rebuilding what you have ruined,

    mending what you've broken

and

it's taking everything you've left of me.

Now,

I'm scared that I will be left with nothing

    once I've undone what you've done.

I was there and not anymore

I kissed the lips of another only to taste yours.

The thing about loving someone so hard – is when
you fail to be,

it's difficult to forget –

and the thing with loving you,

is I could never forget you.

I want to hold your hand.
I want to lie on your chest,
to shower you with kisses,
to hug you,
to share a meal with you,
I want to hear your heart beat,
feel your embrace,
feel your touch,
I want to be with you,
I want to do everything with you –

all over again
-again

Missing Stanza

As I flip another page,

I instantly knew that I can still write a thousand
poems about you,

My ink can still conjure thousands of words to form
similes, metaphors, and imageries of you,

but I think I will never run out of ironies for your
love.

I have then realized that I still have a stanza left for
you,

Even though I try to complete a prose of goodbyes
and never see you again,

I still go back to that one stanza I could never fill in.

No matter how many cinquain or quatrain,

I still revert to the last stanza I could never rhyme.

Flushed by sonnets, haikus, and tankas

I still fall back to the last stanza I could never finish.

For as long as my heart bears the hyperbole of your
inflicted pain,

I know I will never be able to complete the last
stanza.

For as long as the limpid imagery of your promises
still hangs on every corner of my mind,

I will never end the last stanza of your poetry,

For I know that I will only stop writing poems about you,

For I know that my words will stop meaning about you,

For I know my eyes will stop looking for you,

And my heart will stop calling your name out,

If I'll stop writing poems for you

And if my poetry doesn't form your image anymore,

I know I have found a new theme

for my next masterpiece.

Your name

It was 3,

then 5

until it became 10.

These are the number of minutes taking me to remember your name.

When I began to stop thinking about you, my mind suddenly forgot about you and your name.

At first it was taking me 3 minutes to find you in my memory,

then it became 5 and 10 –

and now only your image is in my mind but

the longer the time passes by the longer the

minutes it's taking me to remember your name.

Ironically, instead of being happy –

I feel scared.

I am scared of the possibility that tomorrow,

you have fully departed my memories

and despite the ruins you have left me,

I still want to keep you –

even if it's just your name.

I would know that I'm not there – anymore
when my words can't find
their way back to me – anymore
when my words don't lead
me back to you – anymore

Bitter lies

The cappuccino tasted bitter
   in my mouth
but incomparable
as to when your mouth was
   on mine letting me taste your promises.

2 truths and a lie

It all started with 2 truths and a lie

Never thought that on you I will bat an eye

2 truths and a lie

you said,

I love peanuts

I hate parties

I want to be with you

and yes, you are allergic to peanuts.

2 truths and a lie

you said,

I fell for you

My jeans were tight

The jam tastes good

and yes, you never liked jams like – never

2 truths and a lie

I fell for her

I'm tired

I love you

and yes, you fell for her and you're tired of me – of us

so I stood up

looked at you
reminisced our 4 years together
and for the last time I asked you,

2 truths and a lie
and you said,
I'll be happy for you,
You're free
I love you.

It has never dawned to me how much of my soul you have touched.

How many pieces of me you have taken
and how much pain you have inflicted.

I could never get use to sleeping on the right side of the bed because it was meant to be yours.

I could never drink a coffee with milk because it reminds me of your color on me.

My dreams used to be for two people, but now I can't even dream anymore.

My nights were better, but now they're nothing but nightmares.

Beer used to taste bitter, but now they taste like your lips.

I used to love reading – out loud, but now my voice just reminds me of your eyes.

I used to love and loved so many things, but now I am just hateful and hopeful and sometimes hopeless.

I was just never the same person after you.

Home

Home – it was you.

It was meant to be you.

You are home – the calm in my storm,

my protection, my shelter –

I found you – it was you.

It was meant to be you

but it was never meant to be me.

I was never meant to be your home,

just a transient.

How can you be anything

but

mine?

I hope the next time the night gives me a visit,
your memories will not be the only one that hugs me

—

ok.

I wasn't but it was
the only word I let out
when you decided to
break
up.

You were a shore
and I was ready to be the waves
when you became the sky
and left me,
I was nothing but a vast
ocean of longing and wanting.

Some places are home.

Some places are memories.

Some places are recollections.

Some places are tomorrows.

Some places are painful.

Some places are longing

and some places are

just you.

I never liked the idea of periods in my poems

at least about you –

I hated the thought of ending my stanzas with
periods.

I never fancied the concept of writing with periods
especially about you

because I never want to end anything that has
something to do with you

at least not in my poems

of me

and

you

I was there

right beside you,

I was there

dreaming with you,

I was there

holding your hands,

I was there

in your heart

now,

she is there.

I miss home

And when I say home, I don't mean

the four-walled architecture one built to keep a family
or two.

When I say, "I miss home",

I meant – you.

I miss the warmth you give.

Your hugs were the shelter that covers me from the
storms in my mind.

Your lips were blanket that keeps me from shivering.

Your eyes were the light that guides me every time
darkness kicks in.

So, when I say home, I meant you.

And when I say, "I miss home",

I meant the comfort you bring and the love you give.

You were the most beautiful thing that
has never happened to me.
A story of no ending –
A song without a bridge –
A poem missing a stanza –
A cake without its cherry –
A me without you –
An us without you.

Sometimes my thoughts are still clawed with the idea
that what if I was half as good as her,

Would you still choose her over me?

II. i am here

I've collected all the things
you've given me,
from tears to love
to happiness to sadness
and I've come up with thousands
of letters that will never make sense to you
but worth a thousand memories
for me.

I used to watch the tears fall from my eyes
 with the thought of you.
Now, I watch raindrops fall
 as nature takes me along its course.
I used to pray for your images
 to stop pouring in my mind.
Now, I just pray for the rain to stop pouring.
I used to beg for you to come back.
 Now, I just hope for the sun to come and visit me
every day.

If I were to tell the world about you,
I will tell her that you are the daisies
in a lonely field.

I will tell her that your color is bright red and orange
for you were my sunrise before you came to be my
sunset.

I will tell the world that you were my freedom
before you came to be my chains.

I will tell the world you were my song – on repeat.

If I were to tell the world about you,
I will tell her you were my most beautiful

yet tragic story.

Wanderer

I have always been a wanderer.

Whenever I sit, my mind constantly wanders to places beyond what I can see.

I have always been a wanderer but never of places worthy of photos, but of the scenarios I kept overthinking of.

My mind wanders around every possibility, what ifs, and what will be.

Whenever I flip a page, a new destination arises.

A new question of life and existence occurs as I travel down the path of answers, of possibilities, of answers turned into questions.

My thoughts forming into a train pulling me to places I least expected to be.

At a random time usually at night,

My train of thoughts carries me to memories I never wanted to remember.

Recollections of your vivid image

Anamnesis of our lucid dreams

And before I knew it I'm back to where I was not supposed to be in.

 In your memories.

I have always been a wanderer but never a wonderer.

Dear diary,

Last night, I dreamt about him and it didn't hurt anymore.

Your memories and image are everywhere. I find you in everything and every time I do, it sends billions of bolts in my heart. Pain has become a twin flame of your memory.

But

Last night, after months of suffering, I dreamt about you and it didn't hurt anymore.

The process

Mending an unrequited love takes on many forms.

Sometimes it can be the emptiness you feel right after pouring your feelings to him.

Often times, it takes the form of your forgotten hobbies

which you suddenly started uncovering just divert your emotions from him.

Sometimes it takes on the form of anxiety that creeps to your wholeness as it drowns you

with questions: where did I go wrong? Was I not enough? What's wrong with me? Did I lack anything? Am I not worthy?

But casually, mending an unrequited love offers you the form of those sudden memories of you and him whenever you are alone with the universe.

Though there are times when it's the snug feeling where all you want to do is cover yourself with blanket, close your eyes, and just feel the emptiness.

But there are times wherein mending from unrequited love is nebulous so you can barely recognize that it's actually the regrets, doubts, distrust, fear, anger, loneliness, and bitterness which have been dwelling in the deeper part of your heart.

But mostly it takes the form of a bestial pain that tears your whole existence as it pours countless of fluid from your eyes.

As your emotions berserk into the need of forgetting him – of forgetting the feeling,

It becomes the betrayal coming through your countless night outs and drinking sessions with your friends.

Mending an unrequited love takes on many forms – that sometimes you're forgetting what is the actual form of love,

Because love,

Love doesn't only mean him.

Love comes in the form of the people who hold your hand during your hard times.

Love is the friends you call late at night to cry out loud to them.

Love is your clique who handles you when you've had so much to drink.

Love is the hobby that you always do not because you want to forget him but because you love to do it.

Love is your family who knows you're feeling pain but continue to support you silently.

Love is Him, who took you away from a love who isn't worthy of you.

And love,

Love is YOU.

Your smile, your eyes, your hair, your sneeze, your cough, your wounds, your scars, your anxiety, your drunk photos, your cracked voice, your tears, your pain, YOU.

Love is you dear.

Mending an unrequited love takes on many forms and one of its greatest form is the chance of loving yourself, of finding the truth that there is no greater love than God's and no greater pain reliever but self-love.

What If

For the longest time I could remember, I fought so hard to keep what we have.

I was never raised a warrior but I had to fight for the both of us.

I am not an anchor but I had to keep us from drifting.

I was never the brightest star in the room but I had to keep shining

to keep our love from dimming.

I could not remember when we started to fall apart but the only thing my memory

has was when you finally let go of my hand and my heart.

I wanted to hold on a little longer. I wanted to fight a little harder.

But I cannot.

A soldier who has fought with everything she has, has nothing left but a broken heart.

So the only thing left for me to do was to let go.

And letting go was never this freeing – and liberating.

I never felt so alive, so happy, and so myself when you had my heart.

It feels like my heart was returned to its place – its proper place.

Returning your heart was never easy. Everything we had and we've been through was something

that could never match a treasure

but returning your heart made me felt my own heart once again.

And sometimes, I am just wondering,

What if I didn't let go?

What if I held on?

Will I be this happy?

To patience,

How are you?

How are you holding on with things?

I know you've been battling with time, pressure,
longing, and need

But bear in mind that

'tis a battle only you can fight.

When everything has given up,

Make sure to lengthen whatever you have.

When everything is in doubt

Believe nothing but your own

When you're about to snap,

Remember why you held on for so long.

My dear, you are something that not everyone has.

You are the negligence everyone has forgotten in their
hurried conquest.

Listen to this,

Only a few would understand your presence

And not all will value your existence

But please, stay true to what you are.

Please hold on for a little while.

I'm on my way

Just a little more

And I'll be there.

From,

Love

Favorite book

Just like any other books I've read,

you are slowly becoming one of the "I've read this before but couldn't remember".

you are labeled as the favorite chapter but

now falls under the many favorites.

And just like that, you will eventually belong to

one of the greatest books I've read

but

will be kept under the shelves.

My poems need you, but I don't –

not anymore

If I ever get the chance to choose again, I will choose you over and over again. I would gladly feel and take everything again.

I will trade the last penny I have in this lifetime to go back to the time we first met and I will tell myself, "Hold this man's hand until he lets go."

I will relive all the memories we had – good and bad.

I would gladly go back to our first kiss, first *I love you*, first grocery, first date, first gift, first fight, first doubt, and first tears.

I'll take the chance to once again traverse the streets, corners, and nooks we walked on.

I will once again trace every single line of your body, face, and mind.

If I ever get the chance to choose again, with wide open arms, I will choose you over and over again.

Even with the time you left me shattered.

Even with the time when you brought tears to me.

Even with the time you let go of my hand.

Even with the time you chose her over me.

Because if not for the pain and love, I wouldn't be the woman that I am today.

On the 10th

It was the 11th of the 10th.

I finally decided to cross the road and close the door behind me.

Everything that is and that has been – I've packed them up.

There are still wonders but I've decided to let them be.

You have been and now had been.

The last few moments were teary, but not heavy.

On the 11th of the 10th, I've finally let go of

what could've been to be with what's supposed to be.

The journey has ended

I can finally let go of you.

It took me thousands of courage and two bottles of beer.

I finally got to ask the questions that stood still.

I didn't get the answers, but I got what I needed to know.

It took me three years to let go.

I was running in circles for years –

going back and forth from the past and the present.

Now, I can finally let go of the past to enjoy the present.

I used to be in that place –

It was dark, lonely, a cycle of pain, and full of you.

I was there – in the endless cycle of relapse and trials of moving on

but I am here now,

a present without you

a present filled of hope and just me.

The water is finally calm.
The storm has ended.

The table is about to get cleaned up.
The party is over.

The rain stopped.
The rainbow is showing up.

You're not here anymore.
And I am not there anymore.

I sat by the lake.

I waited for the wind to bring your hand around me.

I waited and waited until the wind has finally caressed my being.

It was cold and unfamiliar.

It didn't whisper anything to me.

It didn't hold me tight.

The wind once again embraced me.

And it was nothing but just a wind.

I was sitting by the beach watching the sunset.

I remembered so many places.

Coffee shops, my room, library, the bathroom, bookstores, the living room, park, hotel, pubs, motels –

All places I've thought of you –

places I've shed a tear, places I felt other's embrace to forget yours, places I've let my thoughts wander for your image.

I've been to so many places after you left me.

I was there for a really long time.

I was waiting for you to come back and take me away just like how you did when we first met.

I did wait and got stuck in that place for a long time

But not anymore

I am here now,

by the water with sunsets reminding me of how beautiful places are – especially the ones without you.

The door has finally closed

I'm bringing you back to the time when you walked away from us.

The day was clear – clearer than what we have.

When you left, I didn't follow or called you, but I left the door open.

I intentionally left it open hoping for you to go back in.

There were moments when I walked out of it to find you.

There were times when I called out to you and you would go back in – for a short time.

It has been the game since I left the door open.

You came in anytime you please.

The door –

it was left opened for a long time that strangers came in rummaging what's left of me.

I let people in hoping they could fill in the space you've left, but all of them have to leave at one point.

I left the door open for you – many came in, but you never did again.

The day I saw you enter another door was the day I conjured all strength I have to finally close the door.

Now, the door is finally closed.

Not just for you, but for anyone who wishes to come in.

About the Author

Emcee Ferrer

Emcee Ferrer is a professional licensed English teacher from the Philippines. She has been teaching English for seven years. Teaching is both her profession and passion, but she's also a writer by heart. She has left her home country in 2022 to explore the world and to gain more experiences in her life, profession, and in love. Before leaving the Philippines, she has been into a really terrible heartbreak which inspired her to write a collection of poems about it.

She recently started a page where she writes poems and motivational essays. Her writings explore ideas about life, love, friendship, adulting, and more. She is a non-conventional writer who prefers to do free writing. She has a very common style of writing which allows most people to relate to what she writes. She is a daughter, a sister, a friend, a teacher, a lover, and most importantly, a woman.

Milton Keynes UK
Ingram Content Group UK Ltd.
UKHW030654130824
446895UK00004B/149

9 789361 726392